CAPTAIN STUMPY THE PIRATE CAT

The Search for Tiggie Pants

By Jeremy E. Bliven • Illustrated by Herbert A. Bliven

CAPTAIN STUMPY THE PIRATE CAT
The Search for Tiggie Pants
Jeremy E. Bliven and Herbert A. Bliven

Published in 2007 by Sir Walter Raleigh Enterprises.

Illustrations by Herbert A. Bliven
Cover Design and Book Design by 8 Dot Graphics

ISBN 978-1-60530-215-7

Printed by Jones Printing, Chesapeake, Virginia

For bulk purchases, special sales and book signings, please contact:
Jeremy Bliven
543 Ananias Dare St.
Manteo, NC 27954
252-475-1442
Jeremy@stumpythepirate.com
www.stumpythepirate.com

The Search for
TIGGIE PANTS

For **ABBY MAE BLIVEN** and **CHASE PATRICK MCGARRY**.

Special thanks to David Guiley

Captain Stumpy, the pirate cat,

and his crew, **GWEN, VAN** and **POP**,

sailed on a pond called the Puddle

away from a fish-house with a shark on top.

They carried a new passenger,

who stood on the bow missing his captain's hat.

It was the **FORMERLY FEARSOME** great ball of fur,

FLUFF BUCKET, the fish stealing pirate cat.

4

Fluff Bucket used to chase Captain Stumpy
just to take his wonderful fish.
But now **FLUFF** and **STUMPY** were the best of friends
and Fluff Bucket only had one wish.

*"We have to find Tiggie Pants before something
terrible happens to him,"* he cried.
Stumpy said, *"I'm looking, I'm looking,"*
and went back to shielding his eyes.

7

Tiggie Pants was the only sailor on Fluff
Bucket's ship, the **"CAT-O-WAR."**
Stumpy sank them with a cannonball,
and Tiggie Pants had walked to shore.

"Me-arrgh!" Stumpy growled as he turned to his crew.
"ALL PAWS ON DECK! *Unfurl the anchor! Heave to!*
We be going ashore Captain Bucket," he said to Fluff.
"And I'd bring some dog biscuits if I were you."

Stumpy's knee buckled just thinking about going ashore.
But he knew he had to be brave
and fight through the **DOGS, RACCOONS** and **OWLS**,
because Tiggie Pants had to be saved.

Meanwhile, the giant pirate, **TIGGIE PANTS**,
sat sleeping in a sunny chair.

A woman attacked him with a broom

and sent him **FLYING** into the **AIR**

She hit him on the head and said,

as she **CHASED** him around and around,

"Get out of here you lion,

or I'll call the pound!"

Tiggie Pants ran until he heard

some kids talking about **SCHOOL**.

He knew that was where all the fish lived

and that made him start to **DROOL**.

He took a seat in the back **and learned some** math,
but his mind was on a **TASTY DISH**.
He raised his paw as his stomach **GROWLED**
and said, *"Me want fish."*

All the kids laughed and the teacher said,
"Lunch time was an hour ago."
A boy leaned over and **WHISPERED**, *"If you want fish
the aquarium is the place to go."*

Tiggie left school and said, **"ME WANT FISH,"**
to the crossing guard standing in the street.
The **OPOSSUM** pointed down the road and said,
"There. But they're for looking at and not to eat."

Tiggie stood and stared at the fish
with his nose pressed against the glass.
He wondered how he could reach those fish,
as he eyed a **TASTY STRIPED BASS**.

Sadly, animal control had already arrived
and searched the building until Tiggie was found.

He was **ARRESTED** at the touch tank,

and taken off in cuffs to the **POUND**.

TOUCH
TANK ⬇

Stumpy, Fluff Bucket and Stumpy's crew,
lowered the **LIFE BOAT** and rowed to **SHORE**.
They all hopped out onto the sand,
and Fluff Bucket let out a roar.

"I found Tiggie's **BOOT PRINT**! *Hooray!"*

Stumpy pointed and said, *"We'll go that a way."*

Their search party walked into the woods,

and the **RESCUE** of Tiggie Pants got underway.

They looked for almost an hour, until suddenly
they came across a **VICIOUS** dog.

It was an ankle biting **YAPPER**,

and everyone except Stumpy hid behind a log.

Stumpy drew his sword and said,

"AVAST YE SCURVY, *land lubbing puff ball!*

I'll give ye a haircut with me cutlass

and leave ye shivering and bald!"

The dog laughed and said, *"You talk funny. And you all dress funny, too. My name's **PYPER**. If I put on a silly hat, does that mean I can join your crew?"*

"ME-ARRGH!" Stumpy growled as he was apt to do.

"There be no dogs in me pirate cat crew."

Pyper looked really sad, so Stumpy said,

"But, I guess you can come along if you want to."

The other cats were not happy about that,

but they all started searching again.

Pyper was so excited, she kept **YAPPING**

and ran around in circles with a big grin.

Stumpy sighed, *"This search be getting nowhere,*
so there's only one thing left to try.
Gwen and I must go up in a plane
and try to see Tiggie Pants from the sky."

Stumpy went to see his brother,
BARON VON LUMPY the flying cat,
and asked to borrow his **RED PLANE**,
a scarf and **LUMPY'S FLYING HAT**.

Gwen and Stumpy started the plane,

rolled down the runway and **LIFTED** into the air.

They flew around and looked for a long time,

but didn't see Tiggie Pants anywhere.

They landed and went to meet

the rest of the **UNHAPPY** crew,

who sat outside the aquarium,

because they didn't know what else to do.

A man opened the door and yelled,

"Get out of here you **PIRATE BRATS!**

Shoo, or I'll call the pound again,

and have you hauled away like that other cat."

They all ran away from the angry man,

and Pyper said with a **FROWN**,

"They've captured your friend Tiggie Pants

and locked him up in the pound."

Stumpy and his crew came up with a plan,

then **SNEAKED** into the pound when it turned dark.

They unlocked the gate leading to the cages,

and all the dogs started to **BARK**.

The cats had never seen so many dogs,
but they had an **IMPORTANT** job to do.
Fluff Bucket took a deep breath and **YELLED**,
"Tiggie Pants! Where are you?"

Over all of the doggie racket
they heard a pitiful **CRY**.
Fluff Bucket looked and saw **TIGGIE PANTS**,
and felt **TEARS OF JOY** come to his eyes.

Fluff Bucket unlatched the lock
and **HUGGED** Tiggie with all of his might.

Pyper asked Stumpy, **"WHAT ABOUT MY FRIENDS?**

Leaving them here just wouldn't be right."

Stumpy thought for a second then spoke
to all of the dogs in the pen.
"If one of me crew gets **BITTEN**,
I'll grab ye by the collar and throw ye back in."

The cats and Pyper let out all the dogs,
who **ESCORTED** the cats to their boat.
To say thank you, they all **BARKED** and **HOWLED**,
which made Gwen hide under Stumpy's coat.

They said goodbye to their new friend Pyper,

and rowed back to their ship.

Pop raised the sails and they started moving

to begin another **PIRATING TRIP**.

"ME WANT FISH," Tiggie said one more time.

Stumpy smiled and announced, *"Let the feast begin."*

They all got a fish, so **TIGGIE**, **FLUFF**, **STUMPY**

and his **CREW**, were all safe and happy again.

CAST OF CHARACTERS

Stumpy

Pop

Van

Opossum

Baron Von Lumpy

54

Gwen

Fluff Bucket

Pyper

Tiggie Pants

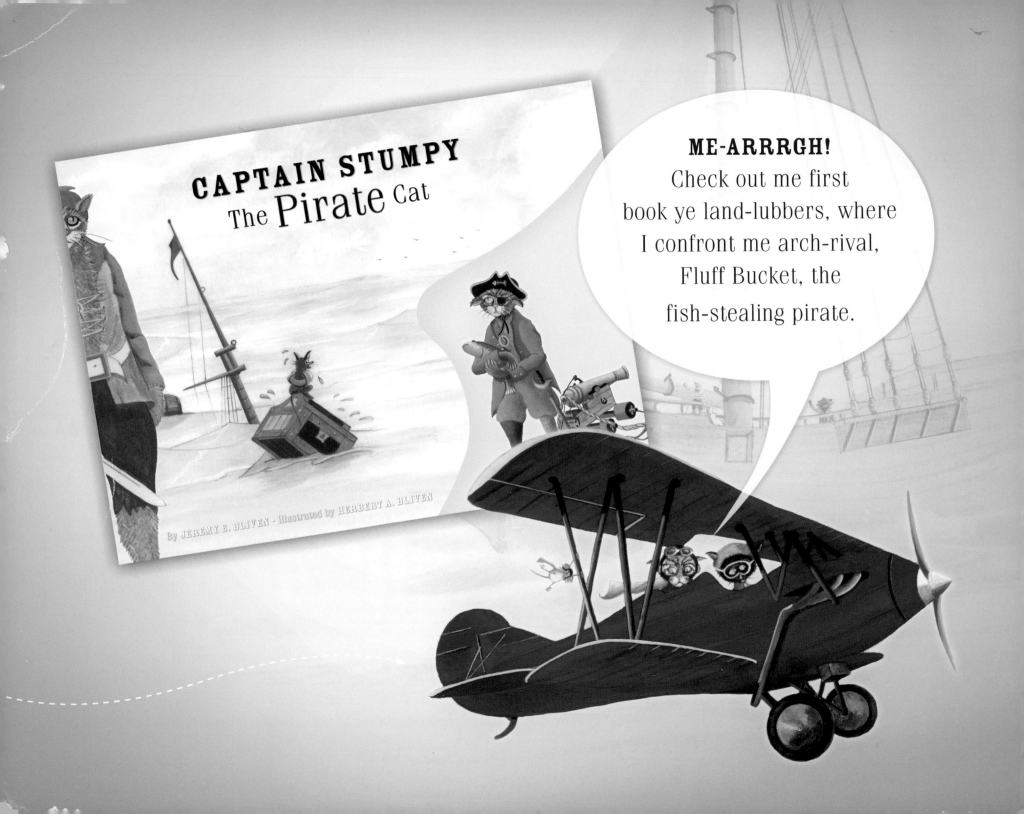